TORN BETWEEN TWO BROTHERS

VOLUME III

(2014 Print Edition)

by

Monique Farrow

Cover Design by: Dzine18

Published by: E-Ink It

Chapter 1

Marcus

I roared down the interstate. Nothing was going to stop me from getting to Fatima. Smacking the steering wheel with one hand, and driving with other, I shifted into fifth gear, and weaved my way through cars. I didn't care if I killed someone along the way. I was on a mission with dire consequences. I would gladly go to prison, or lose my life. I needed to reach my target, no matter what.

"Fuck you! I'm gonna kill you. I'm gonna fucking kill your ass. I swear," I shouted while punching the roof of the car. The taste of salt filled my mouth. Darius was finally successful at breaking me down. I was experiencing a crazed combination of sadness and rage. I couldn't think straight. Since I got his phone call. The tears kept coming. I was an inconsolable mess.

How did I let my pride get in the way? She begged me to stay, but I left anyway. I had no excuse for being so blatantly selfishness. "Lord please, don't take her away from me. I can't live, if she dies," I prayed aloud. "I promise I'll never leave her side again. If you don't take her from me. I swear."

I swerved, and missed a state trooper trying to stop me from speeding ahead. They'd have to do better than that, if they were going to derail my plans. There was no way, a few cops were going to block me from saving the love of my life. A long chain of patrol cars were hot on my trail. They were blaring their sirens, and closing the distance between us. I'm sure we looked like a ghetto set of Christmas lights flying down the interstate. I stuck my head out the window, and saw search lights beaming down on me from the night's sky. They weren't playing. A helicop, and three news stations were tracking my every move.

"This shit was getting out of hand. I had to do something. If I was going to reach her in time."

I stripped off both of my shirts. I threw my navy blue Polo shirt to the side. My white undershirt, I waved outside the window. I wasn't stopping for shit, but I could at least send a peaceful signal. I didn't want any trouble. I just needed to get to her by any means necessary. I veered sharply out of the fast lane, and onto my exit. I was finally out of the city, and onto the dirt road, leading to the abandoned animal clinic.

I checked my rear view mirror, and realized several patrol cars missed the exit. They kept going full speed ahead. The cars near the back of the police chain were able to make it, though. Still, they were a good pace behind me. My brother was the devil personified. He knew how to choose a good place to torture an innocent woman. All the houses out here were inhabitable. It literally was a no mans land, like several pockets in Oklahoma. My headlights revealed the dirt road in front of me, tall oak trees swaying in the breeze lined the street, and vermin scurried in the night.

"I'm coming Fatima. Just hold on. I'm coming. It won't be much longer," I said, assuring myself she was alive.

There could be no other outcome. If she died, I'd be worthless. There was no stopping me from going on a full blown warpath like never seen before. On second thought, that was in the plans anyway. My brother had to die. It was the only way to keep her, and our baby safe. I took a deep breathe, and braced myself. I knew I had to prepare my heart for what I was about to see. Darius told me, I didn't have much time to save her. There was no telling what condition that motherfucker left her in.

The stupid shit I said during our argument early that day, started flooding my thoughts, but I pushed them to the recesses of my mind. Guilt would have to wait. Even worrying about the baby would have to wait, until after she was safe. I couldn't think about what I said, leaving her, or fucking that bitch in the public bathroom, either. Fatima needed me now. And I was going to be there, unlike before.

I tore through the clinic glass door. And sprinted down the hallway, checking every side door along the way. The room at the end of the hall had to be it. I swung the door open, and clutched my stomach at the sight of her.

"Aah! Baby no. No! Look what he did to you," I said, with tears, snot, and spit flying everywhere.

What the fuck did I do? I left her like meat dangling in front of a hyaena. I'm such a piece of shit. I made her pay the consequences for my mistake. How the fuck was she going to survive this shit? He destroyed my baby.

I lifted the throw covering her body. Immediately, I dropped it, and took a step back. Clutching my stomach, I threw up on the floor. She was pieced together like Raggedy Ann. There was jagged and lumpy stitches lining her pelvis from hip to hip.

"I'm gonna kill him. I'm gonna fucking kill him. I'm swear," I said returning to the side of the bed.

I placed my hand on top of her forehead. She was burning up. I checked her pulse, and her wrist flopped down lifelessly. Her pulse was weak, but still there. "Thank you," I said aloud. Fatima looked pale, lethargic, and dehydrated. I lifted her lids, and looked at her pupils. They were uneven, and abnormally dilated. She needed assistance. Asap.

I searched through all the scattered medications on the floor. He obviously went on a rampage, destroying everything in sight, before leaving with the baby. Tears streamed down my face, as I thought about him kidnapping our first child. I killed the negative assault flooding my mind as soon as it came. It would have to wait. Fatima didn't have time to waste.

There was nothing, but animal medications available, but I knew some medication were better than none. So I had to make do with what I had available. Fish antibiotics made by the same pharmacy, I prescribed medications to my kids at the office were laying on top of a pile blue underpads. I crushed five hundred milligrams of clindamyacin between two latex gloves, and put it in her mouth. The bell above the clinic front door rang. I was running out of time. I squirted antibiotic wash, intended for canines, along her incision.

"You're going to make it baby. I got you now. Everything is going to be okay," I said reassuring her, as much as myself.

I took two wash clothes off the counter. I folded one, and scrunched the other. Both, I ran under a stream of cold water. I had to bring her temperature down. The antibiotics would do most of the work by fighting bad microbes and bacteria in her system. But I could still make her more comfortable. I wiped the dried blood off her face, and placed the folded wash cloth on top of her forehead.

I could hear combat boots storming down the hallway, when I was squeezing cold water into her mouth. Fatima was so dehydrated her lips were chapped. And the corners were cracked and bleeding. Light from their flashlights came from underneath the door. I covered her ears in anticipation. I knew they were going blast through like a hurricane.

"Put your hands up, where I can see 'em," a no neck officer yelled.

"Fuck you," I said casually. I ignored him, and continued to squeeze water into her mouth. "She needs medical attention ... I'm a doctor ... and her husband." I stuttered through the last part. In my heart we were married. Even though, it wasn't legal or official yet. I kicked myself for not being a better man when she needed me the most.

"Bullshit! Step away from the girl. Or I'll shoot." He spat back.

There were officers lining the wall outside the room. I assumed they were organizing to take me out, but I didn't care. I was staying by her side. I refused to make the same mistake again. No one was stopping me from riding with her to the hospital. "She was attacked. I had to speed down here, before she lost too much blood, or suffered irreversible nerve damage. I called an ambulance on the way." As if on cue, I could hear them pulling into the parking lot. "Thank god, they're finally here, baby." I kissed her hand, and waited.

"Get away from her," he shouted while walking up to me with a gun, aimed directly at my head.

"Shoot bitch," I pushed so hard against the barrel, I could feel the imprint on my forehead.

A vein popped out of his forehead, and he pulled the hammer back. I elbowed him in the throat, dropping him to his knees. The gun flew across the room, when he reached for his throat. The officer behind him rushed in, and tazzed me. I drug one foot in front of the other, with volts pulsing through my system. I was still coming for his ass. He turned the voltage up, until I collapsed on the floor. I started flopping around like a fish. Officer No Neck got up, and put his boot across my throat. He aimed, and cocked the gun inches from my face.

My life didn't flash before my eyes. No one's did. There was no review of all the good and bad decisions I made. Real life could never be that simple. That full circle shit displayed on television only happens in the movies. Instead. I thought about the last twenty four hours, and the choices I should have made. Arguing about marriage, and moving on was stupid. Why did I think we could move on with our life? We never could. Not with him alive. He'd fight till the end. Now. So would I. I should have put his ass in the ground when I had the chance. That was my only regret. Leaving him alive was a crime against all mankind, but especially Fatima and the baby. I pierced through him with my eyes. If he wanted fear, he wasn't about to get it from me.

"What the fuck is going on here?" Officer Moore busted through door, yelling. "Marcus get on your feet."

Officer No Neck looked down at me, and slowly removed his foot. I called Moore, right after I got the call from Darius. Paramedics worked around everyone in the room. They moved Fatima on a gurney, and started for the door. "I'm going with her," I said, trying to follow.

"Sir, he assaulted and disarmed an officer. He's under …"

Officer Moore put his hand up. "Let him go."

"Sir …"

"I said, let the man go." Officer No Neck muttered to himself, but didn't come towards me.

"You can arrest him, after she is stabilized," he said, looking at me.

I shook his hand, and hobbled pass him, Officer

No Neck, his sidekick, and the cops stacked in the hallway. Fatima wasn't leaving without me.

Chapter 2

Darius

I stared at the live report on the television screen. This shit was more interesting than any action packed adventure, I'd ever seen. My little brother finally got some nuts. He was giving those pigs hell. I sipped on my forty wrapped in a paper bag, and smacked Marta on the ass. She passed me the pipe stuffed with grade A crystal, and returned to take caring of DeMarcus and the baby in the back of the warehouse.

They had his ass on full display. The news outlets posted his full name, his practice address, where he graduated from medical school, and even listed him as a potential suspect. These crackers literally had me rolling on the floor. A potential suspect? My brother? Hell nawl. He may have upgraded those nuts, but he was still on peanut status. Unlike a real nigga like me. He could never step far outside of the box. He didn't have the imagination or testicular fortitude to do something so creative and bold.

I took charge of the situation. He could never do that. He was always so weak and indecisive. Details and potential outcomes, always got him scrambling and unsure of himself. I on the other had, was a like a skilled lion waiting in the jungle. I'd never wait to pounce on a gazelle. I understand the game. He doesn't. Opportunity has always been a bad bitch. She's flighty as fuck, and waits on no man. She knows she has the best pussy around. So you get no second chances, if you're too busy with your dick in your hand. That's it. You lose. Game over. It's done. Lucky for me, he was holding the shitty end of the stick.

I continued to watch, and laugh out loud at the report on the television screen. These clowns didn't know shit. They couldn't put together a lamp, if I gave them all three pieces. They were reporting straight fiction. I had to give myself a pat on the back for doing such a good job.

Marcus Du Bois was the primary caregiver of DeMarcus Stewart, a four year old boy who had been missing for several weeks. Deputies are unwilling to confirm anything at this moment. However, police did discover a body still burning in the back of the building. They suspect the unknown person is the child's mother Tasha Stewart. Personal information was found a few feet from the body, where Marcus arrived on the scene with the victim. Friends of the family say Tasha disappeared several months ago with her three children. Two of them were turned over to the state, after she dropped them off at a local hospital.

Shortly after, she and DeMarcus disappeared. Unfortunately, the hospital reports the unidentified victim found inside the animal clinic is currently in unstable condition.

Stay tuned for more details. We'll keep you updated. Back to you Bob.

I chucked the remote at wall, and it shattered. How did they ID her so fast? I went through Tasha's purse. I had to double check, but I knew her wallet had to be in there. I made sure to put her purse in the car with me, before burning her body. There was a whole bunch of miscellaneous shit inside, but I couldn't find her wallet. Everything was so chaotic that night, maybe I dropped it.

"You know your ass dropped that shit," I voice chided from inside. "You're going to go to jail, you're going to go to jail," another sang.

"Just the fuck up," I yelled, smacking my head. I heard the baby wailing from in the backroom.

"I need some fucking peace and quiet," I yelled to Marta, "Get the baby." I took another smoke to relax my nerves, then shut off the television. I didn't need anymore more updates. What I needed was to think.

DeMarcus ran from the back, and interrupted my thoughts, "Darius, I'm hungry," he said whining.

"What did I tell you about calling me Darius," I

12

roared. He put his head down, but didn't say anything. I knew his punk ass called me Darius to piss me off.

"Can you get me something to eat." He thought he was slick. He still didn't call me daddy, but I had more important shit to worry about.

"Have Marty get you something to eat," I said, shooing him away.

"She won't."

"The fuck you mean? I drown that bitch in dope. She better get you something to eat."

I was pissed. I could still hear the baby crying. DeMarcus wasn't fed, and the warehouse looked like shit. It wasn't even laid. It only had the basic necessities. I converted the office into a bedroom. The garage floor into a living room, and kept the bathroom as is. Other than the television and couch, we only had clothes and food laying around, but she still couldn't keep the place clean. Matter-of-fact, the only thing the bitch did right was suck my dick, and smoke up my shit. That wasn't our arrangement. I stormed in the bedroom with DeMarcus close behind me.

"What the fuck," This bitch had me all the way fucked up. She was passed out with a syringe in her arm. The baby was crying so much, her face was purple, and she was shaking. Her diaper was full of shit, and piss. The room had empty soda bottles, and wrappers scattered all over the place.

"Marta!"

"Marta!"

Oh, she was going to get up. I shook her by the collar of her shirt. "Get up!"

"Huh," she was disoriented, and stammering. I had enough on my mind. I couldn't waste time worrying about her, doing what the fuck I paid her to do. It was simple. All she had to do was suck and fuck when I said, clean our spot, and take care of the kids. Then, I'd give her as much dope as she wanted. That shit wasn't difficult to understand.

"Get the fuck up, Marta" She was still in a daze. Apparently, this bitch thought I was playing.

"Argh!"

I punched her right in the stomach. If she wasn't go to hold up her in of the deal, I considered that shit stealing.

"Stop! Leave her alone," DeMarcus yelled from behind me. Now he was crying.

"Bitch, what did I tell you, huh?" She muttered something I couldn't understand.

Honestly, I didn't give a fuck what she was talking about. I just kept punching her in the face, over, and over again. All I needed was some cooperation. That was it. Every time, I tried to get a bitch to act right, she turned her back on me, or fought against me. Fatima was playing hard to get, like she didn't want a nigga. Tasha was a low budget bitch that couldn't keep her mouth shut. This bitch couldn't follow basic instructions. I stopped short of knocking her ass out, because she still needed to feed and change the baby. If it wasn't for that, I would have got rid of her ass already.

I met Marta on the street, when I was buying my medicine. She wasn't out there long, before I got a hold of her, or at least that's what she claimed. According to her, she started smoking dope, and selling her ass after a nasty divorce that happened three months ago. I believed her, because she wasn't all sucked up, and used looking like a lot of bitches fucking for rocks. I decided to give her an opportunity to get high without being in danger, but she couldn't keep her word like the rest of these worthless bitches, today.

I rested against the wall, and caught my breath. Marta sat up, and staggered to the crib. She started changing and feeding the baby, like she should have been doing in the first place. DeMarcus wiped his tears, and walked up to me.

"Where's my momma?" he asked with a scowl on his face.

"Go play, little nigga. I'm busy."

"Where's my momma?" he said louder. I couldn't help it. I laughed. This nigga was trying to punk me.

"If you don't shut the fuck up, I'm gonna beat your ass."

He wiped the tears off his cheeks with the back of his hand. "When is she coming back? I want to go home."

I had to respect his spirit. He got his courage from me. I handed him a bag of Doritos, and a soda, and told him to go eat, but he didn't walk away. "DeMarcus. Go sit the fuck down, and eat. I'm not playing with your ass."

He bawled up his fist, and started swinging on me. I laughed so hard, tears where streaming down my face. He was really trying to fuck me up. I covered my head, and pretended he was putting in some serious work. My laughter only pissed him off more.

"I know what you did. I saw you. I saw everything. It's your fault my sisters are gone. You made them leave." I grabbed him by the shoulders, and looked him square in the eye.

"You need to chill the fuck out. That shit's over now. You'll be alright. You're just like your old man."

"I'm nothing like you. Don't say that! I hate you.

I wish you were dead. Where's my mom? You took her away from me. You said, she was coming back. You lied."

"So what, I lied, nigga. You ain't about to do shit," I chided.

"Fatty hates you too. Just like I do. She'll never be with you again. My momma told me," that bitch talked about me to my son. Now he thought he could humiliate, or talking about my relationship with my woman.

I grabbed him by his throat, and raised him off the ground. His little head looked like it was going to pop off. Marta stepped towards me with the baby in her hand, but I gave her a deadly look, and she stepped back. I dropped him on the floor, and he broke down crying. His ass should have thought twice about talking shit. Because I wasn't done yet. I pulled off my belted, and started swinging wildly. I covered every inch of his body. Marta, the baby, and he was crying. They all understood who was in charge.

"Marta, make sure he gets something to eat, and goes to bed." I looped my belt, and left the room.

Chapter 3

Fatima

Berenice kept blocking my way with her three hundred pound body. Her short ashy blonde hair, swung in and out of my nostrils. Since, she wouldn't let me pass, and was shaking her head like an excited preschooler. Even though, she was a middle aged woman with a tree trunk frame.

"Oh I'm so excited," she said clapping her hands. "I saw you on television you're a movie star. Can I have your autograph?" she thrusted her note pad and pen in my face. I ignored her, and pivoted towards the opposite end of the room.

Weekly, I was forced to come out of my dorm to interact with the other patients at Saint Mary's Behavioral Ward. I loathed coming out. It was the worst part about being committed. I didn't mind the food. It wasn't great. But it was edible. The staff didn't bother me, and I didn't bother them. So that wasn't that bad either. It was the other patients that drove me up the wall. I just wanted to stay in my room, and read without being disturbed.

I sat in a chair, next to the vending machine. There was a flat screen television on the wall, other residents were watching. I couldn't say what was on the screen, because ever since Darius stole my baby, and attacked me, I avoided television all together. I needed to block everything out. From what I could gather, my story was every. Instead, I watched the clock. It was a quarter till three. I had fifteen minutes before my appointment with Dr. West. I could see Berenice titer tottering over to me. I sunk down in my chair, and covered my face.

"Pretty pretty please. Can I get your autograph, Mrs. Movie Star Lady." I wanted to rip the pen out of her hand, and jam it down ear drum. I chose to take a deep breath. I couldn't do that. She obviously was crazy and special, which was a dangerous combination, in my opinion. Mr. Price, a tall Baluu looking man, walked up, and lead her across the room by the elbow. "Thank god," I said aloud. I looked up, and saw it was three o'clock.

"It's been six weeks since the attack, how are you feeling?" Dr. West asked, but I didn't answer.

He sat across from me at his desk, while I reclined on the leather sofa in his office. It was nice getting out of my dorm room for awhile, without being around the other patients. His office was a welcomed change in scenery. He wasn't too bad, either. He seemed nice enough. I didn't find him threatening at all. He was middle aged, white, and appeared to like his job. This was our sixth session together. The first few times, he visited me in my recovery room downstairs, after my surgery. He was still trying so hard to help me. Even though, I hadn't said anything to him before, and didn't plan on saying anything now.

"Fatima. We can sit here, if you like. But I'd rather help you move forward. We can start wherever you feel comfortable. I know you've been through a lot." I couldn't help laughing.

He jotted something down on his note pad, which only amused me more. I didn't care, if I died inside this place. At least, I didn't have to worry about being attacked, betrayed, or left behind. I was tired of fighting just to lose in the end, anyway. It actually felt like home being here. It was very similar to the shelters and girls homes, I grew up in as a child. Everyone was crazy in there too. We just weren't certifiable. I bet the majority of us were now, though. The thought made me giggle, I'm not gonna lie.

"Staff members are concerned you're not making any progress. They say you haven't been interacting with them, or other residents here. Why is that?"

What the hell would be the point? There was no way anyone could understand me. I was already an odd duck, because I didn't have any family. When you add being raped by your fiance, falling in love with his brother, getting pregnant by one of them, but not knowing which one, being betrayed by your

20

closest friend, and confessing to the man you love, only to get left by him, before his insane brother kidnaps and literally rips your baby out of your body, there was nothing to discuss. The shit was horrendous and unconscionable. So why even try to figure it out? He could never understand the hell I went through. I could careless how many licenses, or degree he had hanging on the wall.

When I woke up in the hospital without my child. I literally lost my mind. I decided to shut down that day. I hadn't said a word to anyone since what happened to me in the clinic. That was their reason for throwing me in this place. I wasn't opening up to anyone, or anything, again. It wasn't worth the risk of getting hurt.

"I understand Marcus has been calling you everyday, still. Why don't you want to hear from him?"

He asked another obvious question, I'm sure he knew the answer to. When I gained consciousness, after my surgery, Marcus wasn't there. The nurses kept telling me he called everyday while I was recovering. How convenient. He called when I was unconscious, but disappeared when I was awake. If what they said was true, that would just be my luck. Regardless. The fact he called, instead of showing his face, told me how much he cared. At first, I believed what he said during our argument was out of hurt, and anger. Especially, when they told me he got arrested after I was stabilized. Since, he wouldn't leave after the police arrived. According to the nurses, half the gifts and flowers suffocating my room where from him. The other half were condolences from considered citizens. It still didn't matter to me, though. I would have rather had him with me at the time. A huge part of me was relieved he wasn't there. Not seeing his face allowed met to forget about him, Darius, Tasha, and the baby. Eventually, I got numb, and stopped hoping he'd show up after awhile.

I hated looking around my hospital room. It felt like I was participating in my own funeral, minus the guests that loved me. All the flowers and cards were so morbid to me. No one I knew was there for me when I needed them most. Shana, Denise, and Trina were sheisty bitches. None of them hos showed up, which made me miss Tasha more than I already did. Did she fuck me over. Yes. Did she fuck the man I loved at the time. She sure did. But I knew, SWAT couldn't hold her back from seeing me in the hospital, if she were alive. One of my biggest regrets was not helping her that day. I replayed our conversation over, and over again in my head. She was wrong, and a piece of shit for drugging me. But I knew Darius was capable of doing anything, in order to get what he wanted. He couldn't have threatened her or her kids. Who knows?

I didn't know why my so called girls didn't show up. Maybe they couldn't handle seeing me in such bad shape. Or maybe the bitches simply didn't care. Truth be told, I didn't give a fuck anymore, anyway. I no longer wanted love, or people in my life. For the first time ever, I didn't give a fuck about having a family, which was a good thing as far as I was concerned. I understood most people couldn't relate to my situation. It was a lot to handle, even for me. To be honest, I did think I could count on Marcus. Obviously I was stupid to think that.

When my doctor asked questions like "how are you feeling," I couldn't help thinking he wasn't qualified to ask me any questions at all, no matter how much he wanted to help me. Obviously, I was feeling alone. Demoralized. And tired of trying to standup, just to get knocked down again. It took more than four weeks to recover from my reconstructive c-section. After Darius butchered me. I still wasn't a hundred percent healed. My incision sight was extremely sore. I still had difficulty getting around. But at least I wasn't strapped to a bed, unable to go to the bathroom by myself like before. I used all my strength to recover physically. I didn't have anything left for my mind. I just wanted to live safely and quietly, by myself.

I could see Dr. West writing at lightening speed on his note pad out of the corner of my eye. I figured the crazier, I seemed the better. At least, I wouldn't have to deal with the hot pile of shit, also known as my life. He put his note pad on his desk, pulled his chair in front of me, and sat down.

"Look. I'm gonna cut the shit, and be real with you right now. Okay?" He hooked his glasses on his shirt collar, and looked deeply into my eyes.

"Life can be a bitch. Believe me. I've been through a lot of shit, too. I'm not going to lie, and tell you I understand how you feel. But I get why you're refusing to cooperate with me. The police told me how you held onto your friends wallet, when you were trapped in the trunk with her body. It takes a strong person to think about someone else, when your own life is in danger. Who knows if they could have identified her body without you leaving that vital piece of evidence." His words pierced a tiny whole through my armor. I hadn't thought about the details of what happened that night. It was too painful.

"I want you to know, I won't discharge you until you're ready. You can speak to me without fear of getting turned out on the street. You're young with a full life ahead of you. You have to believe, you can turn this ship around. Just think about it, okay." He gave me a weak smile, and returned to his desk.

"Thank you," I said, wiping a tear from my eye. It was good to hear reassuring words. I wasn't ready to face my demons yet. Darius in particular. But

24

knowing I didn't have to worry about coming across him, relieved a lot of my stress. I left his office feeling better than when I arrived which was a good change.

Chapter 4

Marcus

"Get up."

A dieseled out looking dude said, throwing his tray down next to mine. He appeared to out weigh me by a hundred pounds, give or take a few. I could tell he was about six inches taller than me too. Even though, I was sitting down on the bench, and he was standing up. I couldn't say, I came across too many men larger than myself. It wasn't surprising to find one inside the county jail, though. The correction officers weren't fazed. They continued chopping it up with other officers, and inmates. It was there would be no rescue team coming my way.

I slowly opened up my chocolate milk, and downed it like I didn't hear anything. Fuck him. I wasn't getting up. If I wanted to get out of jail soon, I had to keep my nose clean though. So I wasn't trying to fight, because I didn't need time added to my sentence, if I was convicted. I still wasn't going to act like a bitch though. My court date was around the corner. According to my lawyer, I'd be free in a matter of days. My status as a doctor, and reputation as a productive and upstanding citizen was working in my favor. Plus, he was trying to get the district attorney to drop all charges due to exceptional circumstances. If I had to go round and round with this fool. It could stop that from happening. Obviously, I didn't want that.

"You think I'm playing with you nigga?" he spat on my back.

I put down my toast, clinched my fists, and stood up. This fool wasn't gonna back down. I flexed, and stepped into his bubble. "What's the problem?" There was no one else at the table. His name definitely wasn't on the seat. He just wanted to try me.

"Hey, what's up baby?" A man with my build and tone, exchanged a handshake with dude, and intervened. I unclenched my fists, and stepped back.

"What up," he responded staring me down, but pushed off.

"Everything good here?"

"Yeah."

The big dude sat at another table. I returned to my seat, and started eating.

"I'm Butter."

The guy who intervened extended his hand, and sat beside me. I shook it, and got up with my tray. I didn't feel like talking, or making new friends, especially not here.

"Wait up." He followed behind me, and dumped his tray too.

I ignored him, and strolled onto the yard. He was only a step behind me.

"I don't get a thank you? What's good?" He threw his hands up in anticipation of an apology.

"Thank you."

"Oh, that's cold blooded." He laughed, and joined me on the outside bleachers.

"No disrespect. I prefer to stick to myself."

"Stick to yourself, if you want to. I'm not stopping you. I was just trying to help a nigga out. This ain't Oz my nigga. Ain't nobody trying to shank you, or nothing." He started to get up. Maybe I was doing the most. I just had a lot on my mind, and didn't need any more trouble.

"You're good." I motioned for him to sit down.

"That's what's up. We're cellmates anyway. You couldn't avoid me, if you wanted to." He laughed.

"Is that right. What happened to Mike?"

"He left this morning. I'm jealous like a muthafucker. I wish it was me."

"Me too."

"I hear you my nig. I hear you."

I hated that word more than anything. Being inside, only made me hate it more. Seeing my own people talk to each other like trash really got under my skin. I couldn't believe, I ended up with the worst of society. I never thought, I'd find myself sitting in jail. That was why I spent all those nights studying, and doing my residency. I was trying to avoid becoming the black male stereotype, people loved to believe. The last year was nothing like I expected. Hell, the last few hours weren't.

I wanted to run through the metal gates guarded the jail, into my car, and straight for Fatima. She hadn't returned any of my phone calls or letters. The shit was really starting to get to me. I spoke to everyone at the hospital. None of them could convince her to get on the phone. In my heart, I knew she was hurting, and having a hard time. I just thought she would be open to talk to me, by now.

The day took forever to pass. I could only watch so many scuffles over fun sized potato chips, and juice boxes. I felt like I was in the second grade again. By the time, it was time to lock up, and go to sleep, I was depressed and exhausted. Butter had the top bunk, and I had the bottom. He wasn't to bad to deal with. In fact, it was interesting to listen to him talk about his life growing up in the corrections system.

He told me stories about doing time for a set he joined as a teenager. You'd think a forty something year old man would have more to be proud of, but he didn't. His face lit up with pride as he reminisced about slinging. He actually considered himself a business man, because he sold eight balls to children and mothers on sleazy street corners. It was disgusting. But it was obvious he had no shame. The funny thing was none of his homies remembered his ass when he got locked up. He was actually surprised. He didn't get any calls from them, or family and friends. But it didn't seem to bother him too much. In fact, he seemed happy. It was obvious, he belonged in jail.

The hallway lights went out, and I climbed into bed with my note pad, and pen. I was ready to get some much needed sleep, but Butter kept talking to me all day. So I had to use the moment of silence to pen another letter to Fatima. Unfortunately, I felt him jump out of bed. How could he possibly having anything else to say? He hadn't closed his mouth all day. I slipped the pen and behind my ear, and pretended to be asleep.

"Mark. You up?"

I ignored him.

He cleared his throat, and said it louder. "Mark. You up?"

I ignored him, again.

"Nigga you hear me. I can see your eyes shaking. Get up. Nigga. Damn." He shook my shoulder this time.

"What do you want? I'm tired."

"I need you to handle something for me." He tugged at the front of his pants.

This fool had me fucked up. If he meant, what I thought he meant. "Handle something for you. What the fuck are you talking about?"

"Look, this is just how shit rolls, inside." He said, grabbing himself again.

"Fuck you. I ain't handling shit." My tongue dried out, and my pulse began to race. Beads of sweat starting to run down my face. I tried to keep a cool head, but I knew I looked nervous. Somehow, I managed to do my time peacefully, with little to no issues so far. Now my worse nightmare was coming true. If this wasn't some Oz type shit, I didn't know what was.

"You gonna handle my shit whether you like it or not. You owe me, my nigga. We can do it nice, or rough. Personally, I like it both ways."

He pulled down his pants, and revealed himself. He was dead serious. I swallowed the large lump in my throat, and got off my bunk. I had to take care of business. He showed me his hand. There was a shank it. He was prepared to fight. I stroked his shoulder to relax him. And he put the shank on top of his bed. I was scared to death. I ain't gonna lie. I didn't know what the fuck to do. He had me cornered. I peaked over his shoulder, and saw the guards standing way down the hallway.

"Don't get any ideas. You'd be bleeding to death by the time they got here."

I knew his was right. They weren't going to put there life on the line for mine. The inmates ran the jail, not them. Their blood ran just as easily as ours. I got down on my knees. I had no other choice. Shit was going down either way.

"Yeah. Handle that shit like a good boy. I ain't gonna tell nobody." He laughed.

I rubbed on his thighs, and looked up at him. I couldn't beat him, one on one. Sure, I was just as tall and strong as him, but he'd been fighting all his life. Instantly, I realized that was the point of telling all those stories earlier today. He was letting me know, he knew the game. He let out a sigh, and rubbed on my head. He pulled my mouth closer to him, and I put in work.

Aagh!

He started swinging, but I got the jump. I slipped the pen out of my pocket and stabbed him, over and over again. Blood was spilling from the main artery lining his groan. He was bleeding out, fast. I could see the guards running toward our cell from the other end of the hall. I was knotting him up, and digging my hands into the gap I created above his thigh. The audacity of this nigga. Yeah, I called his ass a nigga, cause that was exactly what he was. I found a new appreciation for the word.

"He attacked me," he cried, holding himself. The guards threw me onto the floor, and radioed, I was going to seg which was fine with me. I'd be damned, if a nigga thought he was gonna turn me out. I'd just have to deal with the consequences. I was more than happy to go to segmented administration with my cheeks, and manhood completely in tact.

*****

"We have to stop meeting like this." Officer Moore said, shaking his head.

I was isolated, and kept behind a steel door. The correctional institution considered me a high risk inmate. Nothing could've been further from the truth. As long as, people kept their distance, I was good. He spoke to me through the tiny window, at the top of the door. Somehow, he got word of my situation.

"We don't have to meet at all," I said. Why the hell, he was even here? I didn't get it. I was grown enough to understand what I did. I didn't need a man, who has never been in my situation slapping me on the wrist.

"Don't get lippy with me. I'm here to stop you from destroying your life." He was genuinely pissed. He face turned different shades of red, faster than I thought possible.

"Excuse me, I didn't know you cared." I laughed, not caring for the conversation.

"Listen to me, you fucking idiot. I put my neck on the line, for you. James called my office, and told me about your situation. I personally took time out of my day, to speak to the district attorney, who happens to play golf every week with my father in law. I was able to convince him to drop the charges. But then you turned around and did this stupid shit."

My face dropped. I didn't know what to say. I really felt like an idiot. "Thanks anyway," I muttered.

"Luckily, I was able to still get you out of here. The DNA results came back from Tasha Stewart. It matched the Good Wife Killer case files. I'm sorry we didn't believe you and Fatima. We should have."

I didn't feel like I should. Why wasn't I jumping up and down like a won the lottery.

"You don't have anything to say?"

"That's good news I guess."

"What the hell are you talking about? That's the news of the century. We can finally nail that fucker." He was looking at me like a second head was growing out of the side of my neck. "Oh forget. You're getting discharged tomorrow morning. Keep your ass out of trouble. I'm not helping you anymore."

Officer Moore walked down the hallway shaking his head. He wanted something I couldn't give him. In my opinion, it wasn't good news Darius was on their radar. I wanted to kill him, myself. Jail and lethal injection were both too good for him. The only thing he deserved was death by my hands. I looked forward to personally delivering his sentence.

Chapter 5

Fatima

"What is he doing here?" I asked, pointing to Marcus. My therapist completely betrayed me. I told him how much I needed to be alone right now, but he invited him to my session anyway.

"Fatima. Believe me. It's for the best. Everyone needs a support system to get back on their feet. Who better than Marcus to support you through your recovery? He's the person that can understand your situation."

He couldn't be serious. Marcus was sitting in the trunk with me, and Tasha's broken down body. I don't think so. I was in there suffering alone. No one else was in labor, laying beside me. He was gone somewhere, blocking my calls, because he couldn't handle my past mistakes. I wouldn't say he was able to understand my situation at all. If he could, I wouldn't have been alone when Darius got me.

Marcus sat across the room with his head down. He was visibly uncomfortable. I wondered, if he even wanted to be here. His body language was closed off, and unsure. He didn't even try to make eye contact with me when I came into the room.

Apparently, he knew I was pissed.

"You lied Dr. West. We had an agreement. You promised to take things slow, until I was ready."

"I didn't lie to you, Fatima. You've been making significant progress. Staff tells me, you've been interacting more, and showing steady signs of growth. I want to encourage you, and keep things moving in a positive direction by nudging you outside of your comfort zone. I promise, I'm doing this because I know, it will help you."

I folded my arms, and stared across the room. I wasn't going to win this battle. So I stopped trying.

"Marcus. Do you have anything you want to say?" He gave him an encourage smile. I did my best to counteract it by twisting up my face. Whenever he wanted to say, I wasn't going to make it easy. He certainly, didn't make life easier for me, or my daughter that day.

He cleared his throat, and sat up straight. "I hate the circumstances. But it's good seeing you again. You look beautiful as usual." His eyes were soft, and pleading. I didn't want to hear anything he had to say. It was too little, too late. At this point, nothing in the past mattered to me anymore.

"Can we cut to the chase please? I don't want to do this. Trying to get over what happened was bad enough without you dragging me back to the past."

"Fatima. I know this is hard for you. But Marcus is a survivor as well. You two can be a great strength to each other. I don't want you guys to rehash the bad things that have happened. Instead, I need you to take the good out of the situation. So you can better move forward."

"Take the good out of the situation, huh?" I laughed. He couldn't be serious? There was no good, in the situation. Unlike, everyone else, I saw the full picture, including the frame. Marcus could paint himself as a victim while trying to find the right angle, but it wouldn't change anything. The reality of the situation was he avoided me when I was in labor, and needing his help. As far as I was concerned, he was only a lick better than Darius.

"Maybe this wasn't a good idea," Marcus stood up to leave.

"No. Please sit down. You're doing great. I know how much it took for you to come here." Marcus sat back down, and Dr. West directed his attention toward me. "This has to happen. Whether you realize it or not, things aren't going to get better by avoiding the situation."

"Fine. I'll participate. He needs to know how I feel anyway." I sat on the edge of my chair, and peered across the room. "The truth is I loved you, Marcus. I really did. I trusted you. I thought you'd protect me, and that we'd be together, after my baby was born. Note. I said, my baby, because you made it clear, she wasn't yours. Not that she's already gone, and there's nothing to show for my life, I don't want to see you, or even hear your name. Do you know what was happening to me, when you were blocking my calls? Do you?" I was yelling now. They wanted to hear the truth. So I was going to give it to them.

"That's good Fatima. Let it out. Marcus, what do you have to say."

"I'm sorry. What else can I say? I'm sorry, I said those awful things to you. I'm sorry, I didn't answer my phone. I'm sorry I wasn't there for you when you woke up. I'm sorry for everything you've been through. If there was anything, I could do to change the way things turned out, I would in a second." He eyes welled up with tears.

To my surprise, he wasn't trying to defend himself, or make up excuses. I felt so dumb. I was speechless.

"Good. I'm glad you were both able to get everything on the table. Is there anything else, either of you want to say?"

Marcus spoke up. "I want you to know, I still love you. I don't care about what has happened in the past. If you give me a chance, I'll prove how much I love you, and our daughter. I'm willing to wait, if you want me to."

After all the horrible things I said to him, he still wanted to be with me. I couldn't wrap my mind around what he said. So I stayed quiet.

"Did you hear what he said, Fatima? Do you want to give your relationship, or friendship, another shot? It seems like there's still a lot of potential there."

My heart wouldn't buy the lies my mind was selling. I could yell, and scream all I wanted, but I still loved him. Seeing his face again, made me think of our daughter, and the life we could have had. "I don't know, if I can do that right now." I told the truth. Even though, I missed him, I wasn't ready to be vulnerable again. I still felt like I was walking around with no skin on.

"Take all the time you need, babe." He sighed, and flashed a big smile. I grinned too. I think we both felt a huge weight, lifted off our shoulders.

"Before we end our session. Marcus had some news he needed to share with you." Dr. West motioned his way.

"Oh yeah, I almost forgot. I was so happy to see you again. It slipped my mind. Officer Moore was able to match the DNA results found at clinic with the victims of the Good Wife Killer. They're finally updating his records. Darius is a wanted man now. And not just by the state." His face changed when he said his name. It was obvious he hated him, as much as, I did.

"See Fatima. Even in a desperate situation, you were able to help strangers you've never met. The family and friends of those victims are enormously grateful. Think about all the woman, who won't come across Darius when he's found. You still have a lot of strength, and life left. You just have to find it again."

"I'm glad, they're looking for him now. I'll sleep a little easier tonight."

I really noticed Marcus for the first time during the visit. He didn't look like himself. His eyes were low, and tired. It appeared he picked up a few crows feet since the last time, I saw him. Maybe Dr. West was right. He didn't experience the same things I did, but he certainly was a victim. The thick scar wrapped around the front of his neck, wouldn't let me deny the pain he'd been through. He must have seen the pain, and softness in my eyes, because he walked over to the couch, and hugged me. He held on to me so tight. I thought I was going to burst. It felt so good to be in his embrace again. Instantly, I remembered all the good times we shared.

"I shouldn't have attacked you. I'm sorry." Before I could stop the words from leaving my lips, they were already out there. Marcus successfully disarmed my defenses by being kind and

41

understanding, regardless of the blows I sent his way. Now I felt embarrassed, because I planned on never speaking to him again. My behavior was unreasonable. It wasn't hard to tell who the immature, and unforgiving person was in the room.

"None of that matters now. I'm just glad to see you." I looked into his deep brown eyes, and began to cry. Why didn't we fall in love, and live happily ever after like the stories I read as a child. He was such a good man. We deserved a fairy tale ending. He wiped the tears from my cheeks, and kissed them. "I want you to know, I'm going to get our Briana back. No matter what happens, I swear. I know she's out there. I can feel it. Darius wouldn't hurt her anyway. Because she is his most valuable chest piece." He whispered, "I'm gonna get him, before the police. I promise you'll sleep peaceful every night."

"Marcus …" Even though, the tension in the room disappeared. He placed a finger over my lips. I could only assume, he felt my apprehension. I was going to tell him don't bother looking for Darius. I was finally ready to accept my situation. It was nice seeing him, and getting closure, but I still wasn't ready to confront Darius having our daughter.

Chapter 6

Marcus

I debated whether or not to go inside. My mom's doctor said, she was having another manic episode, and kept calling for my father, Darius. Since, I was the only living relative she had left, besides my brother of course, the responsibility fell squarely on my shoulders. I hadn't seen her in over a year. And honestly, I wasn't looking forward to seeing her now. Things weren't bad between us. It was just too difficult to see her in such bad shape. She didn't remember me half the time, and when she did, she never had anything positive to say. It was like her mind only kept record of the traumatic, and horrible events that occurred in her life. It was simply too depressing to deal with.

I decided to man up, and go inside, anyway. I pressed the call box, and waited, "Yes?" a voice called over the intercom.

"I'm here to see my mother "Lu Ann Du Bois," the intercom buzzed, and the gates opened. I made sure to put her in the best home money could buy. If she was too ill to live with me, I at least wanted her well taken care of elsewhere. I drove pass the stone lions guarding the entrance gates, and made my way up the wrap around driveway. The attendee took my keys, and parked the car, before I entered the nursing home double doors.

"Can I help you?" I small blonde asked from the nurses station.

"Yes, I'm Marcus Du Bois." Dr. Cashing called me earlier today. She suggested, I come visit my mom Lu Ann, because she's been having regular episodes lately.

"Oh you're hear to see Lu Ann. Bless your heart," she said, giving me a sympathetic smile. "Come this way sir." She lead me to the back of the facility. It was beautiful outside. There was a nice waterfall right through the court yard entrance. It ran into a pond full of water lilies, and other floating plants. As we made our way to my mom, we passed an assortment of exotic perennials, garden stones, and humming birds feeding from their dishes. It was like stepping into Snow White's backyard out here.

"There's she is," the lady said, pointing to my mother sitting on a cement bench feeding some squirrels.

"Thanks," I replied. She looked as beautiful as I remembered. She was still tall and slender. Her curly salt and pepper hair was wrapped into her signature french roll, she always pinned with a silver dragonfly comb my grandmother gave her.

44

"Hi my mom," I said, sitting beside her.

"Oh Darius. They finally called you." She threw her arms around me, and held on tight. "I thought you'd never come."

"I'm not Darius. I'm Marcus mom. How have you been doing?"

"Don't be silly, Darius. I know who you are. Did Sally get those cookies, I made for the church bake sale? Me and Marcus stayed up making them all night. He's such a good boy." She bent down, and fed the squirrels as she talked. A huge grin swept over her face.

It broke my heart to see her so happily confused. I didn't know what to say.

"I want to thank you for being so good to me. You didn't have to stay with me, after what I told you."

What was she talking about? I'm sure I didn't know all my parent's business, but I wasn't aware of any major secrets. I wanted to know more information.

My mom stopped feeding the squirrels, and came to sit beside me. She grabbed both my hands, placed them in her lap, and looked deeply into my eyes. "You didn't have to accept Darius as your son. But you did, because you're such a good man. After what my daddy did to me, I thought nobody would

45

want me. I appreciate you taking me in." She patted the top of my hand when she spoke. It was obviously difficult for her to say.

After my visit with Fatima, I couldn't stop thinking about my mom. Looking back, she really had her shit together, especially considering her background. At least, she had it together before Eric passed away. She seemed more impressive now, because I didn't know my grandfather assaulted her.

She was an excellent mother, despite her upbringing. Every morning, she would put me and Darius on the school bus with Eddie wrapped tightly around her waist. We would get bum-rushed with kisses and hugs before she sent us off. Of course, other kids on the bus made fun of me for being a momma's boy. But I didn't care. To me, she was the most beautiful woman in the world. Her beauty was only out-shined by her generous heart, and love for me. Fatima reminded me of her, so much. Before she was attacked. It was one of the many reasons I fell in love with her. Unfortunately, they were more similar than I would like for them to be. They both withdrew, when life got too rough.

As a kid, my little league coaches would volunteer to take me home after practice. Just so they could find a reason to speak to her. They knew she was married, but that didn't stop them. They even tried to buy her affections by spoiling me, and my brothers, with candy and toys. She never accepted their advances or gifts. Somehow, she managed to deny them without bruising their egos, or causing bad blood. She really was a class act. You'd think all the men stiffing around would keep my dad on his toes, but it didn't. Maybe her huge revelation about my granddad, fathering Darius was the reason for his coldness. Growing up, he seemed too arrogant to care about any of us, but especially Darius, and my mom. He never appreciated the fact he had a good woman waiting for him at home. I'll never understand why they stayed married so long. Neither of them seemed happy. How they lasted until his death would always remain a mystery to me. Most of the time, he was too busy to be bothered with us, because he was chasing after half the congregation. He hardly noticed my siblings, or mom. I guess her survivor's guilt stopped her from ever straying, or divorcing him.

"You know he is just like him," she said, starring off into the distance.

"Little Darius?" I asked, making sure I was following.

"Of course. Who else could I be talking about? He is always getting into trouble. Every time I turn around, I'm getting a phone call from the school, church, or neighbors. The boy never settles down. I tell you, he's a bad seed. I shouldn't have had him." She shook her head as she recalled old memories.

47

I never heard her speak ill, about any of us. Not even after what he did to Eddie. I actually was angry at her for a long time, because of it. I couldn't understand why she didn't get mad at him. She just lost her mind, instead. After it happened, my dad kicked Darius out of the home. He told her, he had to go, or he was leaving. They ended up sending him to juvenile facility, anyway. But it wasn't long before he went awol.

"Every thing will be okay," I said, rubbing her back. She was obviously getting distressed.

"No it won't. You know it won't. You tell me all the time, you regret giving him your name. If I knew, what was going on I could have stopped all this from happening." She cried.

"Calm down." I tried to console her, but she threw me off. She was really getting worked up.

"No. Stop it. I'm tired of hiding this. Why didn't I know what was going on. It happened to me."

She really had me confused now. What was she talking about? My grandfather couldn't have been the problem. He died shortly after Darius was born. "Earl is dead." I said, trying to help clear her thoughts."

"I'm not talking about Earl, Darius. It's Larry, I'm talking about." she said with a scowl on her face.

"Larry? What does he have to do with Darius?"

"Oh god," she wailed. "I could have stopped it. I should have known what was going on."

The nurses in the courtyard started looking our way. I gave them a look that said, I had everything under control. I wanted to know where she was going. "Go on," I said, patting her back.

"It was a day like this. The sun was shining. The birds were out. Everything looked so beautiful. Then I saw it. He was on top of my boy. The bastard! The bastard!" she screamed. "How could he do that to a little boy?" she slapped her lap in frustration. "I pulled him off, but it was too late. Darius was laying on the ground bleeding. I picked him off the ground, and wrapped him up. My baby was never the same. He died that day. I should have killed my brother."

I wrapped my arms around her. She was a complete mess, now. I said, I love you, and kissed her cheek like I did as a little boy. The staff had to intervene. She was too upset to continue the visit. It was time for her to go back to her room. I was still glad, I came to see her. Because everything about my childhood became clearer after our conversation. No wonder my dad didn't want to stay home. He was reminded about what happened to her, and Darius. Our conversation also explained why she never let anyone talk bad about Darius.

Even after what happened he did to Eddie. The whole town knew what he did, but the police couldn't prove it. So, she didn't want to hear a word about it. I guess she felt what happened to him was some kind of excuse for his insanity.

As far as, I was concerned. One thing had nothing to do with the other. So, he was still in my sights. I had no intentions of letting our beef go. I rubbed my hand across my scared up neck. I was still putting his ass down, regardless.

Chapter 7

Darius

The last few days were a bitch. I couldn't leave my crib without dunking and dodging like a rat caught in the Matrix. My face was plastered everywhere. The other day, I heard the state was offering a hundred grand for information leading to my arrest. A hundred grand for little old me! These pigs weren't playing out here. They wanted my ass bad.

Naturally, I was on edge. I felt like all eyes where on me, because they were. Today, I went to get some food for me, Marta, and the kids. I should have been able to send her out with a few dollars, but the bitch couldn't be trusted with fifteen cents. So I had to go out, and get the shit myself. I thought I was going to get caught today. Since, a little girl pointed me out to her mom. I was at the chink store, up the street, at the time. Minding my own business, and ordering the usual. I asked Abib, or whatever his name was, for a couple of blunt sticks. So I could roll up some cush and ice, when I got home. This little girl was tugging on her mom's leg the entire time I was standing in line. She kept asking, if I was the man on television. I'd never been happier to see a hoodrat in my life. Her mom was a racket ass bitch that wasn't paying her no mind. She actually told her to shut the fuck up. I couldn't believe it. God was showing me favor. If she was decent, my ass would be locked up right now, or wetted up with lead in my chest. I couldn't have been happier to get home.

As soon as I walked through the door, I could hear the baby crying and screaming in the back room. Where the fuck was Marta and DeMarcus? I slammed the door behind me, dropped the groceries, and stomped through the house. Something was definitely off. It was easy to survey the area, unlike at night. The utilities had to go. I couldn't afford to have noisy contractors or utility workers walking around my property. It was too big a risk. Especially with DeMarcus, and the baby living here. I had to let a lot of comforts go which was starting to wear me down. This bitch couldn't carrying her weight, which wasn't make shit any easier. I was needed to get this bitch in line. Apparently, she thought I was playing.

I walked to the back screaming their names, but no one answered. When I swung the door open, I was livid. The baby was on her stomach struggling to breath, and Marta was passed out high, with a needle in her arm. I was enraged. I picked up the syringe, and started stabbing her with it. I bet the bitch would wake up now. She screamed and cried as usual. I was done playing game with her ass.

"I'm sorry. I'm sorry." she cried. "I didn't mean

to fall asleep."

I knew her ass was sorry, now. She was rolling back and forth on the bed, sobbing. If she did what I said. There wouldn't have been any problems. What the fuck am I paying her to do? She had the best job, a smoker could ask for. All she had to do was watch the fucking kids when I was gone. And the bitch couldn't even do that, simple shit? I didn't feel an ounce of simple for her stupid ass. I had better shit to think about.

I flipped baby girl on her back, and realized DeMarcus wasn't in the room. Where the fuck was his ass at? Doubled back to the front room to get the formula I bought, and threw at Marta while she was crying on the bed.

"Feed her. And change her baby too. I have to go find DeMarcus, you dumb bitch." She nodded, and reached for my baby. I slapped the bitch like she was crazy. "Clean the fuck up first. Damn! Do I have to tell you everything. I headed out to find my son. He couldn't have gotten too far away.

I crept down west side OKC with my arms stuck in the front of my hoodie, and the hood pulled down as low as it would go. It probably wasn't necessary, because the area was filled with society's waste. There was nothing but crackheads, homeless people, and strays on the street. Anyone brave enough to walk out here alone, didn't give a fuck about their life or safety, let alone who I was. It was serious out here on these streets. Still, I decided to take the extra precaution anyway.

Was that his little ass, pushing the shopping cart across the street? It was. He had on the same jacket and jeans he wore, before I left for the store. He had me fucked up, if he thought he was running shit. I jogged up behind him, and grabbed his shoulder with my good hand. He spun around, and screamed so loud, I grabbed my ears. "Get off me, motherfucker!" He yelled. "I don't know you, cuss."

This bastard wasn't my son. There were people outside, chopping it up and slinging. They looked up, and turned in my direction. I knew none of them gave a fuck about what a did, but a hundred thousand dollars was a lot of reasons to call the police.

A Fat Albert look-a-like looked directly at my arm. I tried to shoved it back in my hoodie pocket, but it was too late. "Hey, Nick. Ain't that nigga, wanted? I know I saw this fool on the news last night." He nudged the short skinny man smoking a Black & Mild standing next to him.

"You right, my nigga. That's him." He turned towards the house and yelled, "Yo, Bird. Get my cell phone. It's on the side of the bed."

I hooked around the trigger in my pants pocket.

The other three men in the yard flashed their steel, before I could. I decided to let it go. I couldn't win a gun fight. I was at least three against one. Instead, I spun on my heels, and took off in the opposite direction. They hoped in the car, and peeled out of the driveway. I needed to get my ass home. I was running like a new slave trying to break free. I ended up hiding in a commercial trash can, for at least thirty minutes. They weren't trying to me. The saw dollar signs on my ass.

When I got home, I stunk. Every inch of my body was soar. My blood was boiling. The voices inside my head wouldn't shut up. I was angry, and ready to kick some ass. The warehouse was spotless, and quiet for a change, but I didn't give a fuck. This bitch risked my freedom. There was no forgiving that shit. But before I dealt with her, I needed to take care of me.

"Baby you hungry?" She tiptoed in the room with the baby on her hip. "I made you a plate. Do you want it?"

Did I just hear this bitch correctly? She couldn't have said, what I thought. My calculated plan was falling apart, because she couldn't watch the kids for thirty minutes. And she asking me, if I want a fucking sandwich. I broke down the blunt with shaking hands. I needed to smoke more than ever. "Get the fuck out of my face." She ran in the room with the baby.

I hit the blunt, and choked. That shit felt so good. My blood and bones relaxed, instantly, for the first time all today. Finally, I was in the right frame of mind to make some logical decisions. My thoughts weren't jumbled, and all over the place. If I was going to stay out of jail, and get Fatima back, I had to come up with a plan B that would correct the problems Marta created. First, I needed to jot down all the mental pros and cons. Pro. Fatima wasn't fucking with my brother anymore. That much I knew from writing my peeps in jail. When I got the news, he took out Butter. I actually, swelled up with pride. I never thought Dr. Do Right could survive a stint in jail. Let alone with a hardcore nigga like Butter. I paid good money to have him turned out. Apparently, I underestimated my kinfolk. Pro number two. Baby girl was still with me. She'd be the perfect bargaining chip I'd need to bring Fatima crawling back home. I ran out of pros faster than I thought. So I decided to hit the blunt again. But at least it was a start.

"This nigga must be crazy. Pros and cons? There ain't no fucking positive side to this shit." a voice said, from across the room.

I jumped off the couch, and started swinging. "Who the fuck said that?" looked under the couch, and around the room.

"Is everything okay, baby?" Marta rushed into the room with baby girl in her arms.

"I admit you were right." another voice answered.

"Yeah, nigga. I told you. Pay up. This fool is going to jail." Where were the voices coming from? They didn't sound inside of my head. I thought someone caught me slipping, but I was alone.

"I ain't going no fucking where." I screamed at the top of my lungs. They were trying to trick and confuse me, but I was too smart for that. They never won before, and they weren't going to win now.

"Baby, calm down." Marta put baby girl on the opposite hip, and rubbed my back and shoulders.

"Give me my child," I snatched my daughter away from her, and she started crying. I didn't want this dumb bitch anywhere near her.

"Darius, I'll leave you alone, just give me the baby back." She actually looked sincere, but I didn't trust her. My daughter was wailing, and screaming like I was a stranger. I couldn't figure out what was wrong with her. I tried bouncing her up and down, patting her back, and rocking her back and forth, but nothing was working.

"What the fuck did you do to her? You turned her against me." I yelled, pointing at Marta. I couldn't believe this bitch. She was setting me up at home too.

"Fuck you nigga. She sees right through your trifling ass. That's why she's freaking out." Tasha rolled her neck, and sucked her teeth. What the fuck was she doing here? She pushed her hands against my chest.

"Get off me. Get off me." I shrieked. Still, she kept walking towards me. "Back the fuck up, Tasha." She wouldn't leave me alone. Her face was burned, and crusted just like I remembered. I didn't understand. How could she be here?

"What's the matter nigga? You can't say hi to a bitch. Where do you think your going?" she taunted.

I flipped out. Between her nagging voice, and baby girl's cries, I lost it. I kicked her in the stomach, and started stomping her. There was no way, she was taking me out. Blood sprayed me and baby girl in the face, after every blow. I couldn't stop, until she was a puddle of mush, on the floor.

Chapter 8

Marcus

Thanks to concerned citizens a missing four year old boy was discovered, earlier today. DeMarcus Stewart, the son of the Good Wife Killer's latest victim, Tasha Stewart, was found in downtown OKC. Two good Samaritans responsible for calling police are live with us now. We'll check in with Dan for the latest details.

Thanks Patrica,

I've been standing here with these two very observant and upstanding citizens, in disbelief. Please explain, how you managed to spot him on this very busy intersection beside us, during the middle of the day?

"I was just chilling wit my girl, when I saw him walking down the street by himself."

"Uh huh, this ain't no safe area for no little boy."

"Ya mean. We just glad he got somewhere safe. And didn't get hit by a car. You dig."

"Well there you have it. I don't know about you guys at home, but I'll sleep a lot better knowing he is safe, instead of on the streets. Back to you,

Amy."

I closed the window on my web browser. I couldn't believe the good news. My nephew was actually alive, which meant little Briana probably was too. I pulled out my phone, and dialed Officer Moore. Even though, he said, he wouldn't help me again. I knew this situation had to be an exception.

"Moore's office," the receptionist chirped through the phone.

"Hello Misses …"

"Taylor."

"Ah, Misses Taylor. What a beautiful name. This is Dr. Du Bois. I was hoping to speak to Officer Moore. Is he in?" I made sure to emphasis doctor. Hopefully, it'd be enough to push me through without any questions.

"He's not in right now." Damn. He must have told her to block me.

"Please Miss Taylor. Patch me through. It's not about me. I really need his help."

"Hold please."

Yes. I got through. Elevator music started playing. Then I heard, a clicking sound. "Officer Moore," I asked, failing to hide the excitement in my voice.

"What do you want?"

"I don't mean to bother you, but I need a favor."

"A favor. You've got to be kidding me. Have you started smoking crack in between patients. You must not remember our last conversation.

"Whoa, whoa, whoa. Here me out. Before you jump the gun. The favor isn't for me."

"Just come out with it, already. My line is blowing up."

"The little boy they found today on Prospect and 23rd street is my nephew."

"Your nephew, huh. Why am I just hearing about this? You do understand, we're in the middle of an investigation involving a serial killer, who just happens to be your brother, right?"

"Would you like me to send a screen shot of the cord wrapped around my neck?" I didn't hide the indignation in my voice. I needed his help, but I wasn't about to let him forget who knew the situation up close and personal.

Officer Moore cleared his throat. "I'll ask you again. What do you want?"

"I want to adopt him."

With laughter in his voice he said, "Well son, I can't help you with that. You're barking up the wrong tree."

"You may not be able to help me, adopt him.

61

But, you can put in a good word with the social worker on his case. I want to be his foster parent. Your recommendation would speed things up. He's been through enough already. It's really the only plausible option."

"Is that right?" he said, sarcastically.

The line went dead. I nervously rubbed my head, and awaited his response. I needed to make sure DeMarcus was okay. That was the least I could do, considering I was the only sane relative he had left.

"I'll see what I can do, but I'm not making any promises."

I muted the phone, and jumped up and down in excitement. "Thanks man, you won't regret putting in a good word for me, I promise."

"It ain't for you. It's for the boy." He hung up the phone, before I could thank him anyway.

Shortly after talking to him, I received a phone call from a social worker. She needed me to come down, and fill out some paperwork. It just so happened, the shelter was overcrowded, and few foster homes where available at the time. The shelter actually started accepting toddlers, and newborns which was typically against protocol, because the system was so overwhelmed. So, she was more than happy to help. DeMarcus was coming home with me. I just needed to rush downtown to pick him up.

Getting him discharged didn't take long at all. I signed on the dotty line a few times, and he was ready to go. When they brought him downstairs, I was shocked at his condition. I couldn't help staring. He looked awful. His eyes were sullen, and dark. I needed to do a double take, he looked like a little prisoner. It was obvious, he'd been through his own personal hell. He held his face like an old man, not a child. The innocence was gone from his eyes.

"He's ready to go." The old woman who brought him downstairs said, looking hardcore. She smiled, but it didn't seem genuine. I was glad, he wouldn't be spending anymore time with her. "He doesn't have any clothes or belongings to take with him. You should call his worker. Maybe, she'll be able to give you a clothing voucher. The poor child doesn't have anything. Bless 'em." She said, shaking her head.

DeMarcus held his head down, and played with his fingers. I didn't want him to feel ashamed. "That won't be necessary. We're going to buy brand new clothes, shoes, and toys just for him."

"Really," he exclaimed. His eyes lit up, and he started jumping up and down like I did, after I got the good news.

"Really," I replied. I got on his level, and stared into his eyes. He was starting to look like a little kid already. "You ready to go?" I asked, extending my hand.

He nodded, clasped mine. A few minutes later, we were driving out of the parking lot.

On the way home, I stopped and bought him a happy meal, and an Oreo McFlurry. He was so happy. He couldn't stop smiling. Then, we stopped and picked up some clothes, hygiene products, and a few toys from Kohl's which sent him sailing over the moon. When we got back into the car. He was strangely quiet. Until then, he'd been talking since we left the shelter. Concerned. I asked, "Are you okay?"

He nodded but didn't turn in my direction, or say anything.

"You know, you can tell me whatever you want. And I can't say a word, because you're my patient." I said, while paying attention to the road.

He shook his head.

Why are you shaking your head?

"You're not my doctor. Now you're my dad, right?" He asked.

"Technically no." Immediately, he shoulders slumped, and he started to look sad.

"I'm you're uncle though." He crossed his arms, and turned his knees toward the door.

"I'll still take care of you like a dad. What do you think?"

"I hate him. If his my dad, I don't want one." I was surprised he had such strong feelings about Darius. I wasn't even sure, he knew who he was.

"You don't mean that, do you?"

"Yes I do. He's mean. I wish he was dead."

"What did he do to make you so angry?" Of course, I could totally relate. But I wanted to understand where DeMarcus was coming from. They interviewed him, after he was found, but they didn't get anywhere. He said, he didn't know to every question they asked.

"He made my sisters go away. I don't know where they are," he said with tears welling in his eyes. "He took my mom away too. I hate him. I wish he was dead."

If only he knew, how much I agreed. I pressed on, for more details. "When is the last time you saw you're dad?"

"He's not my dad!" he yelled. This time tears were streaming down his face.

"I'm sorry," I said, taking my hands temporarily off the wheel. I could totally understand how he felt. I didn't even claim him, myself. "Did you see him, a long time ago?"

"No. I saw him yesterday." He sniffled, and whipped his eyes. I wasn't sure, he understood what he saying.

"How long ago was yesterday?"

"You know what yesterday is," he crossed his arms, and looked at me like I was crazy. "The other morning. You know. Before you woke up, today."

I had to give it to him. The kid was smart. He was little, but smart. He understood, exactly what I was saying, which got my wheels turning. Maybe, he could lead me to Darius. I could rescue Briana, and kill him, if I knew where they were.

"Can I ask you a question?"

"Shoot," he answered like a little man.

"If I drove around to different buildings. Could you tell me which house Darius lived in?"

"Yeah," he nodded again.

I wanted to take him driving around, right now. But it was already ten o'clock. His eyes where low and heavy. His little head kept nodding forward. Then, he'd sit up, right before falling asleep. "Do you want to go home, now? Or do you want to help me find Darius, the super villain, like a superhero? We can help save the day, and call the police, because he is one of the bad guys?" I had to lie, and make it sound exciting. I couldn't risk him forgetting where he lived. I refused to miss such a great opportunity. The news broadcast, showed where they found him. Darius couldn't live more than fifteen miles from where they interviewed the two eyewitnesses.

"I want to be a superhero!" he exclaimed.

"Good. I'll buy you another ice cream, after we find the house." I figured a little motivation couldn't hurt.

"Yay!" he cheered.

We both were excited, and fully awake. At first, I had no idea, how I was going to find Darius. I was beginning to lose faith. I never imagined, god would send me such a little helper. But I was sure glad he did.

Chapter 9

Fatima

Her lips were black, and looked like leather. I didn't want her in my room. She gave me all types of Cleo vibes from Set It Off. Actually, that was inaccurate. Even Cleo looked soft compared to her. Honestly, she was the hardest looking woman, I'd ever seen. I didn't want to judge, but I couldn't help it. Her appearance screamed cookie snatcher. I didn't know how I was going to sleep with her lying next to me in the room. As soon as she came in the room, she was mugging.

Dr. West tried to warn me. He said, it was about time I got a roommate. Since, it was the only step left, before getting discharged. Reluctantly, I agreed. He obviously wanted me to take a leap of faith. I decided to brave it, but I wasn't expecting someone like this. Maybe, he thought we'd automatically connect. Since we're both black girls. I knew some white folks thought, we all got along. If that was his assumption, he was way off track. I planned on talking to him about my new living conditions, during my next session. At first, I thought Darius was the only person I feared. But the way my mouth dried out, and my pulse started racing, I was starting to think I was fooling myself.

She started cackling, and I jumped.

"Damn you're a scary ass bitch." she said, plopping her things down on the bad.

"Excuse me?"

"Oh. I see. You're one of those siddy bitches. I should have known. You look like the type." She sat on her bed, and crossed her legs at the ankle. Apparently, I wasn't the only one, judging a book by it's cover.

"I'm not siddy." I stuttered.

"I'm not siddy," she mimicked. "Even you're voice sounds like a white girl."

"Whatever," I moved to the opposite end of the room. Picking up my book along the way. I drug my chair in front of the window, and tried to read, but my nerves wouldn't allow it.

"If it makes you feel any better. I think you're kinda cute."

My stomach twisted into a thousand knots. I knew, she was a cookie snatcher. I threw my book on the floor, and shot up. I needed to draw the line. "Look. I'm not a lesbian. Whatever, you got swimming around in your head. Ain't gonna happen."

She started slapping her leg, and laughing like I told the funniest joke, she ever heard. "If I was a cookie snatcher. You couldn't stop me anyway. I can see you shaking, and sweating from here."

I wiped my forehead with the back of my hand. Damn. I was such a coward. Of course, I was nervous. I crossed my fingers, and hoped she couldn't tell. Unfortunately, I wasn't so lucky.

"Calm down, Hilary. I won't steal your cheeks." she wiped away happy tears, and extended her hand in my direction.

I really didn't want to take it. I didn't appreciate her making me out to be an ass. But I did anyway to keep the peace. She kissed it, and I snatched it back.

"You can give it to me, though. If you want," she started laughing again.

"Uh huh, this shit isn't gonna work." I stormed towards the door. They needed to find me a new roommate.

She jumped in front of the door, and put her hands up. "Wait. Damn. I'm sorry. I was just fucking with you okay."

It appeared, she was being honest. But I didn't care. I just wanted her to get out of my way. I tried to move past her, but she pushed me back. "Bitch, are you fucking crazy?" My adrenaline was pumping now. Was she really trying to keep me in my room.

"Look. I said, I was sorry. Please don't call staff." I could see tears welling in her eyes.

The door opened, and Mr. Price entered the room. "Is everything okay, in here?" he asked, looking between us.

Her eyes plead with me. Now she was the one sweating bullets, and looking nervous. I didn't know what to say. I wasn't trying to stir up shit. I just wanted her to keep her distance. "Everything's fine," I said, looking her square in the eyes.

"Hey, we're good." she put her arm over my shoulder. Immediately, I threw it off.

"You sure, Fatima? He asked again, looking concerned.

"I'm okay," I smiled.

"Let me know, if you'll have any problems." He left the door opened, and walked out the room.

"Damn girl. You're cool people. I thought you were going to sell me out."

"Sell you out. What are you talking about. You're the one acting crazy."

"Aren't we all." She said, laughing again.

I looked at her like the fool, she was acting like. I was right about her liking girls, but this chick was a mess. Everything that came out of her mouth was a damn joking. She was really getting on my nerves. I screwed up my face, and went to sit down. She got up, like she was going to try to shut the door, again.

"What are you doing?" I asked, spinning around.

"We need some privacy?"

"No the hell we don't. If you need privacy. Go to the bathroom. Whatever you need to say, go ahead, and say it. But there's no need to close the door." I crossed my arms, and rolled my neck. She was going to fool me again.

"Man, forget it. I was going to tell you why I got in here. But you probably don't care anyway."

I really was getting antsy inside this place. After Marcus came to visit, we started talking again. My mind started wondering what it would be like to get out. Sitting by myself in silence wasn't doing it for me, anymore. I could really use a good story to break up the boredom. "You can close the door." I sat on the side of my bed that was facing hers.

"Cool." she shut the door, and returned to her bed. "Damn this is awkward."

"You got your way. Now you don't want to tell me why you're in here." I asked, annoyed.

"Nah, that's not it. I really didn't want anybody to know. It's not the easiest thing to talk about." Her demeanor changed. She looked shy, and uncomfortable. I'm sure that wasn't normal for her, considering how loud, and rowdy she was acting before.

"Then, why the hell did you bring it up?" This woman was really starting to get on my nerves. Hell, maybe I didn't want to hear a good story after all. I really wasn't trying to pull teeth. Suddenly, I realized I didn't even know her name. And she didn't know mine, either. "Why don't we start with basic introductions. "Hi. My name is Fatima," I stretched out my arm. "What is your name?"

"I knew you were fancy." She sucked her teeth, and shook my hand. "Hi Fatima. I'm Donn." She said, smiling.

I wasn't surprised by her name, at all. She looked like a Donn. Not the type you'd find beautifully rising over the clouds, but the one you'd find on the corner selling rock. I could only imagine what she did to get in here.

"Now that we got that out of the way, tell me why you're in here?"

She fidgeted with her clothes, and rolled her neck. She sure was acting dramatic. "I killed my baby daddy." She said it so fast, I wasn't sure I heard her right.

"What did you say?"

"Damn girl, keep up. I said, I killed my son's father." This time she stretched it out, like I was

73

slow.

I got up, and started pacing the floor. She was worse than I thought. Now, I really didn't want to share a room with her. "Oh." I said, trying to hide my judgment. The last thing, I wanted to do was piss her off.

"So now you're going to start acting funny."

"Uh huh," I lied. "What makes you say that?"

"You're pacing back and forth like a rat, trapped in a corner."

"Did you just call me a rat?"

"Don't change the subject. Admit it. You look at me differently now."

I put my hands on my hips, and stared her down. I didn't think much of her to begin with. "Tell me why you do it. Make me understand. How can you hurt another human being. Especially, someone you loved."

"Shit. Your ass is too damn naive. I wish my life was as simple, and good, as yours." she said, rolling her eyes at me.

I grunted, and looked away. She could tell her business, but I wasn't sharing shit with her. "It's not my place to judge anyway. That's between you and god. He'll have the final say."

"For someone who's not judging me. You sure

sound like it. Why you got bring god into it, and shit. I bet you don't even have no kids."

Her words hurt. Lately, I'd been thinking about Briana everyday. At first, the psychotropics and my fierce denial tricked me into believing I was ever pregnant. But after, Marcus came, and we started talking again. I couldn't get her out of my head. I started thinking maybe, she was still alive.

"You do have a child." She said, reading my thoughts. "You look good girl, you can't even tell." I appreciated the compliment, but not the look. She was staring me down like a box of milk chocolate. Her eyes sent shivers down my spine.

"Yes. I have a daughter. Her name is Briana." I was surprised, she didn't hear about me on the news. "Here's a picture of my son," she pulled out the photo, beaming with pride. He really was a cute little boy.

"He's very handsome." I said, smiling.

"Thank you. Can I see a picture of your daughter," she asked, expecting me to reach in my pocket.

"I don't have one."

"Yeah right. I see how you is."

"For real. I've never seen her before."

"You've never seen your own child. What kind

of mother are you? You had me fooled. I thought you were one of those church types." Her eyes told me, she couldn't believe what I said. "I could never give up my child," she continued. "I'm in here, because they let me out early for attempted murder. I say I killed him, because he might as well be dead. I got that motherfucker good when he was sleeping. He's in the hospital sucking on a tube. I heard his mother is trying to decide, whether or not to pull the plug." Her face lit up like a Christmas tree. There was no denying she was proud of what she did.

"Why are you here, instead of the prison. Some people get life for less."

"Oh my case was exponential." She said, misspeaking. I'm sure exceptional, was what she meant. "I came off from work, after speeding two hours on the bus. The motherfucker forgot to pick me up from my job. When I came home, I didn't see my son anywhere. The house was quiet, and spotless. I was actually grateful, he did something while I was at work for a change. When walked into the bedroom. I found him on top of my son. He jumped out of bed, and tried to sooth me. My mind was reeling. I didn't know what to do. For the rest of the night. It was like I was in a different world. That night, we all went to bed like nothing happened. Except, I couldn't sleep. I walked down the hall, and peeked in my son's bedroom. To my surprise, he was asleep. In that moment, it hit me. It wasn't the first time, that happened. All those times, I was at working pulling doubles, he was chilling at home, raping my son. I walked to the kitchen in my night gown. I did my best to stab him into tiny pieces. Then, I picked up the phone, and called my sister. After, I told her what happened. She called the police, and picked up my son. The rest is history."

It may sound crazy, but I was proud of her. There wasn't any shame or hesitation in her voice. Her fierce protection, and love for her son, told me what I needed to do. I had to get out of here.

Chapter 10

Fatima

I smiled, and took in the view. Finally, I was getting my mojo back. I placed my shopping bags on the hotel floor, before climbing onto the kind sized bed with my box of treasures. During my stay at Saint Mary's Behavioral Ward, I received hundreds of letters from people reaching out to support me. One of the only positive things about being attacked was I learned how supportive complete strangers could be. I was amazed at their generosity. If it wasn't for all their donations, I wouldn't have been able to afford this room. In total, I received twenty three thousand dollars to get on my feet. Thanks to a fund drive ran by a local church and family owned bank. A bag of thank you cards sat on the floor for every person who wrote me while I was too sick to take care of myself. I couldn't appreciate them before, because I was too hurt and damaged. Today, I was proud to say I was ready to face my past. The next thing on the agenda was apartment shopping.

Most of the letters I read said the same thing. They prayed for me, wished me well, and encouraged me to have faith in finding my daughter. The last bit was already true. After meeting Donn, I realized I couldn't give up on myself, because I would be giving up on her, if she was still out there. Initially, it was easy for me to accept she was dead. It eliminated the possibility of getting hurt again. For the same reason, I planned on keeping Marcus at a distance, but now I completely changed my mind. If our daughter was out there. She needed us, and I had every intention to be there. In fact, I'd been trying to get in contact with him for the last few days, but he wasn't answering his phone.

The next envelope, I planned to open, read from Dimples. Immediately I started to shake. Swallowing down the lump in my throat, I prayed out aloud, "God please don't let it be him." I flipped the envelope over, and opened it. I was shocked to find there wasn't a letter inside. Instead, I found the backside of a photograph.

Hey, Fatty

It's me. You're love, and future husband. I thought you'd like to see, how our baby girl has grown.

I love you,

Dimples

P.S.

Don't be stupid. She wants to meet her mommy. It's been too long. If you give me any reason to think you're trying something slick, unfortunately, you two will never meet.

See you soon.

Tears covered my cheeks, and bumps ran down the length of my body. There was an address listed at the bottom. There was also an offer expiration date at the top right hand corner. His deadline was tonight. "Thank you god," I cried aloud. Even though, she was with the devil. My baby was still alive. I quickly flipped it over the pictured. Instinctively, I gasped, and dropped it on the floor like it was on fire. My baby girl was drenched in so much blood, I couldn't see her features. What the hell was he putting my her through? It looked like she was screaming her head off. I couldn't tell if it was hers or another person's blood. I had to get to her, asap.

My ring tone went off beside me, in the bed. I glanced over, and saw it was Marcus calling. I was too messed up to speak to anyone. I sent the call straight to voice mail. I had to clear my head. I prayed, god answered me quickly. I needed guidance, and solutions to get my Briana back. Involving police wasn't an option. And staying away wasn't either. I was going to be there, no matter the danger to myself. My tears where full of joy, excitement, and pain. I just wrapped my mind around being with Marcus again. Unfortunately, our rekindled relationship would have to wait.

*****

I stepped outside the yellow cab with a set of
shopping bags full of baby items. I set them on the
sidewalk, and double checked the address on the
back of her picture. In disbelief, I realized this slum
was it. I grunted in disgust, and waved off the taxi.
Doubtful thoughts rushed into my mind. I should
have called the police, my subconscious screamed
in the back of my head. What if it was a trick, and
she was already dead? I shoved the thoughts away,
and picked up my bags. I already lost her once, I
wasn't going to risk losing her again. Standing on
the sidewalk, I knew I made the right decision, the
doubt only set in for a second. As if living on the
west side wasn't bad enough, he had my baby
sleeping in an abandoned warehouse. Getting her
couldn't wait for police, or anyone else. She needed
me days, weeks, even months ago. I felt shame for
not getting it together fast. Strolling up to the
building, I noticed it was blacked out, and crowded
with so much trash, I couldn't tell if Darius was
home. The seedy neighborhood made me feel
apprehensive enough. The lack of streetlights,
opened businesses, or signs of activity only made
me more nervous. Still, I approached the front door.

Before I could reached it, a man walked up

81

behind me, "Hey shorty. Can I get some change off you."

I clutched my shopping bags and purse. He looked to be about twenty five. Apparently, he wasn't too old or proud to beg. I ran through my options. I could give him a few dollars to make him go away. Money really wouldn't matter anyway, if I had to live with Darius. Or I could tell him to get lost, and take my chances.

"Get the fuck out of here," I jumped back, and looked behind me. The voice I never wanted to hear again sent shivers down my spine. Darius held Briana in his hand-less arm. He pointed and cocked a gun at the stranger.

"I'm cool brother. I don't want no trouble." He put his hands up, and backed away.

Briana started to cry, and everything disappeared around me. I ran, and snatched my baby from him. She was so beautiful. She looked like a little me. I gave her my finger, and she quickly grasped it. "Hey pretty mama," I said, kissing every part of her body. I couldn't see through my tears of joy. That moment was everything to me. I waited so long to see her little face, I couldn't stop crying and singing her praises. Darius was a forethought as I strolled up to the front door. I was completely lost in the moment.

"You look good, Fatty." He said, bringing the

bags inside.

Even in the night's sky, I could see he looked much worse than I remembered. He wasn't the strong tower, I met years ago. He's clothes weren't clean, and crisp. His Cesar cut was missing. It looked like he hadn't cut his hair in months. The stink coming off him was almost too much to bare. But, my love for Briana was strong enough to endure his presence. To my surprise, I wasn't possessed with fear. For almost a year, I created every worse case scenario in my mind. I was convinced, I would fall apart, if I ever came across him again. Amazingly, fear didn't overtake me. I wasn't shaking with fear, but I was hot with anger. The worst was behind me, he had no power left. I was willing to anything to set things right.

Sitting on the couch in front of the kerosene heater and lamp, I scanned the coffee table in front of me. He was keeping track of every story with my name, or face on it. I felt a cold rush over me, but it wasn't from the cold draft inside. Darius was finally playing his last card. So far, the deck was completely stacked against me. I needed a distraction. The lack of electricity was going to make it difficult to catch him off guard. There was nothing in the room to steal his attention from me. Still, I was going to figure something out, because me and Briana weren't separating ever again.

Darius placed the items I bought onto a shelf

standing against the wall. I watched him balance foil on his wrist from a cross the room. He dropped a rock on top with his good hand, and fired up. He was definitely dedicated to the cause. He eyes rolled into the back of his head as he inhaled.

"Ooh wee, that's that good shit right there," He rolled his neck, and joined me on the couch. "Fatima, why don't you get a little taste? I promise you'll like it." He said, nudging the drugs my way.

I put Briana on the couch beside him, and started changing her diaper. "Thank you, baby. I'll have to try some later. Briana needs a diaper change, and looks really hungry. Besides, I want to spend as much time with her as I can. We've been apart for so long." He looked at me sideways like there was a devil and angle on each shoulder. God only knows what was going on inside his head.

"You've missed her, but have you missed me?" He asked with wide eyes. I knew telling the truth wasn't an option. I had to buy time.

"What do you think?" As much as it pained me, I pecked his dry lips. My stomach curdled thinking about all the possible things he pressed against them. They weren't sweet and supple like they used to be years ago, before lost his mind. Instead they were dry, rough, and worn like him.

He moaned happily, and took another hit. A small peck on the lips wasn't going to keep him satisfied for long. I had to act fast. I knew, Darius didn't debate or argue. My mind drifted to the night, I lost my best friend, Tasha. For some crazy reason, he treated me different than his other victims. If I was anyone else, I'm sure he would have killed me by now.

"Damn girl. I'm so happy you're home. I was beginning to think I'd never get my family back, again." He broke my thoughts as I finished, changing Briana's diaper. He yanked me to the side, and pulled me in between his legs. Briana was cooing, beside him on the couch. I made eye contact with her to avoid staring into his eyes.

"Look at me." He grabbed my chin, and said, "I love you." His eyes board through me. He was obviously looking for signs of deceit.

"I love you, too." I smiled weakly, and prayed my act was convincing.

He held me tight, breathed in my hair, and said, "Fatty, I can't wait to taste your sweetness. It's been so long. You don't know, how long I've been waiting for us to be together, again."

Thank god, he believed me. He released his grip, leaned back, and started tugging at the front of his pants. I knew, exactly what he wanted me to do. Images flashed through my mind of past abuses. The thought of him being inside me, shocked my system.

He placed my hand on the bulge in front of his pants.

Licking my lips, I mocked desire, and unbuttoned his pants. He rubbed his chest, and stared me down in anticipation. I have to do this. I have to do this. I might as well get it over with now. He stood up, and I sat on my knees. Looking up at him, I slowly unzipped his pants.

"Open your mouth," he said pulling out his monster.

The thought made me gag, but I couldn't show it. I obeyed, and pulled him to me.

The sound of tires rolling, came from outside. "Damn. Who the fuck is that?" he said, pulling up his pants, and scurrying across the floor. "Get down," he shooed me towards the baby, then pointed towards the door in the back. I sighed, and dropped my shoulders in relief.

Chapter 11

Marcus

Finally. The day of reckoning was here. DeMarcus was an awesome sidekick. He pointed out the abandoned auto shop with ease, a few days ago. I paid a local freshman up the street to watch him while I did what I needed to do. At first, I thought about calling Officer Moore. The publicity I received involving Darius, and his attics knocked several zeros off my bank account. I really didn't want to lose anymore. Besides, he helped me so much in the past, I almost picked up the phone. I also thought about turning around, because I didn't want to risk my practice and reputation. I worked so hard for both. But then I came to my senses. Darius was a big fish, I deserved to catch. On second thought, he was a piranha that deserved to die for almost taking my life, stealing my child, and destroying the woman I loved, and our relationship. I rubbed my neck, as an unfriendly reminded of what I needed to do.

I rolled into the back of the warehouse parking lot with my lights, and engine shut off. I peered through my tinted glass windows, and noticed flickers of light beaming through the warehouse. He was home. I quickly tucked the handgun sitting on the passengers seat in the back of my pants. Before, leaving the house I made sure to strap a holster around my waist. I carried another gun on my hip as backup. Getting out of the car quietly, I patted my hip down confirming my backup piece was snugly at my side. Then, I reached for the nine inch blade strapped to my ankle. I wasn't going to underestimate him by going into battle unprepared.

I grabbed the 9mm from my side pocket, and lurked up to the building. The parking lot was wide, and empty. The only thing breaking the silence was the sound of gravel shifting underneath my steel-toed boots. I switched off the safety, and peeked into the window. I could see candles, and a kerosene lamp from the window. I couldn't see much else, the room looked empty besides a beat up looking couch sitting in the middle of the floor. I slide to the side, and slowly reached for the door.

"You make it so easy." Darius said, with laughter in his voice. He shoved me against the door, and started jumping around the empty parking lot like we're two little kids playing freeze tag.

"You think this is a fucking game." I said, seething with anger. He was jumping around like a fool.

"Life's a game, my nigga. You're just too stupid to realize it. Maybe that's why you stay losing." I could see he was enjoying egging me on. "If you took the time to learn the rules, maybe she'd be with you, instead of me." He said, wearing a mischievous grin. He threw his hands up, and started laughing.

What the hell was he talking about? I knew he couldn't be talking about Fatima. My finger clung to the trigger in my hand.

"Yeah, nigga. It's exactly what you think. My woman came to her senses, and chose the better man. She was actually preparing to suck my dick, before you rudely interrupted."

I fired in his direction. I didn't want to believe what he said. Me and Fatima were just starting to get back on track. He slide across the parking lot, and he ran by the side of the building with a gun in his hand. I pivoted, ran, and crouched behind my car. We were both out of sight from each other. "I don't believe you. Fatima wouldn't do that. She always was too good for you."

"Yeah, keep telling yourself that," he jeered. "Just remember, she never left me. I gave her to you."

"You never gave her to me. She made a decision. She couldn't handle living with your crazy ass." I said, peeking my head over the hood of the car. He fired. I jumped back, and fell on my butt. I scurried to my feet, and heard him laughing. He wasn't taking me seriously.

"That's your other problem. You're a bitch. I hate to tell you that, but it's true. Women don't want a paper tissue nigga. Why do you think they stay choosing men like me over you?" He paused for dramatic effect. I wasn't going to respond. I didn't show up to have meaningless conversation. "Fatima came back, because she respects me. She may not like my methods, but it makes her enjoy the dick even more when I'm plunging deep inside, because she has something strong to hold on to. Meanwhile, a bitch like you is at home with tears on your pillow. You're out of your league, my nigga. Throw in the towel. I really don't want to hurt you. Already had to kill one brother."

A sharp pain pierced through my back. I dropped my gun, and reached for my side. Darius picked up the gun I dropped, and stood over me.

"I told you. Go home. You're out of your league."

"Why are you doing this?" I asked, gripping the deep wound on the back of my hip. It felt like a six inch blade went through me. He came out of no where.

"Don't play innocent now. You did this. You should've let Fatima go."

"Why do you keep bringing her up. This isn't about Fatima. You need to stop. You can't keep taking people out. You've been doing the same shit, since we were kids." It was true. Fatima, and the baby were my main motivation. But I also had other people like DeMarcus to think about.

"And you think a bitch like you, is going to stop me?" He gave me a pitiful smile, and circled around me. I hated how much he was enjoying seeing my down.

"If you're gonna kill me. Do it. Why keep fucking around?"

"Oh. I'm gonna kill you. That much, you don't have to worry about. I just want to stretch it out. You're brother. I want to make this moment special." He grinned.

He threw both guns across the parking lot, and started stomping me. I covered my head, and managed to kneel while taking the body shots. I wasn't going to back down, or going out without a fight. I came way to far, already. I pulled the gun out of the back of my jeans, and fired. Darius grabbed for his ankle with his missing hand. He started hobbling away.

BANG! BANG! BANG!

I kept firing, and missing. My clip was empty. I so threw the gun to the side.

"I underestimated you again." He said, laughing out of breath. "Just like I did with Butter."

Instantly, my heart started thumping harder

91

against my chest. There was no way he could have known what happened. "I didn't come here to talk. So shut the hell up. I have no idea what you're talking about."

"Oh, don't lie about it. You should be proud. My ears told me exactly what happened. From what I understand, he had you bent on your knees. Just moments before he put his dick in your mouth, you got the bright idea to stab him."

He waited for a response, but I didn't give him one. He could think whatever he wanted.

"You know I sent him to you, right?"

"Shut the fuck up, Darius." What was he talking about? How could he access, Butter from outside without getting caught.

"You remember my man, Eddie don't you? Well, he owed me a little favor. When I heard you got locked down. I had him place the order with Butter. He was supposed to make you his bitch."

I wish I was surprised, he could stoop so low. But nothing he did could ever shock me. My blood was still boiling, though. I regularly thought about that day. He was going to pay for what he did. "I don't believe, you were trying to hurt me, Darius. In fact. I think you wanted me to know how good you felt when Uncle Larry was plunging inside you."

He screamed. I heard him running my way,

before I saw him. "Fuck you! Fuck you!" he yelled, throwing heavy blows all over my body. "She told you. I can't believe, she told you," he cried.

I was so weak and dizzy, I could hardly move. Darius rolled beside me onto the ground. Tears were streaming down his face. He was wailing, and sobbing out of control. In all the years of my life, I never saw him cry. I'd be lying, if I said, I wasn't hurting for him. Even though, I hated him more than any person in the world. I felt bad, he went through that shit. I kept my eyes closed, and slowly reached for the knife strapped to my ankle. I got it. In one swift move, I rolled on my side, and stabbed him in the neck.

He screamed out in pain. I got on my knees, hooked my arm under his, and raised him by the wound in his neck. He cries got even louder, but it didn't stop me. I was going to put him out of his misery. I slit his throat from ear to ear. I sick joy enveloped me. I finally won. Darius rolled on his back, grabbing his throat. His eyes were wide in shock. Exhausted, I fell against the back of the car, and pulled out my cell phone. I took a few moments to catch my breath. Then, I stood up, and called Officer Moore. I had some good news, I wanted to share with him.

"Hello," he croaked, sounding asleep.

"It's Marcus."

He grumbled into the phone. I couldn't help laughing.

"What do you want? It's 3 o'clock in the morning."

Fatima stood in the door with our daughter strapped to her hip, I mumbled, "I'll call you later," and hung up the phone.

"Oh my god," she gasped, and wrapped her arms tightly around my back. I flinched, then she loosened her grip. "I'm sorry, baby."

"Don't worry about it." We walked slowly inside. She sat on the couch while I took everything in. Finally, life was going to be good again.

Fatima screamed. And I turned around. Darius was standing at the door with a gun in his hands. He pulled the trigger, but the gun jammed.

"Duck," Fatima screamed. She threw the kerosene heater over my head. It exploded in front of me, and caught him on fire. I fell onto my back. She pulled me away. Darius was howling in the flames. We both watched silently, until he died. My phone started ringing, again. Fatima answered on speaker phone.

"Have you lost you're rabid ass mind? Don't you ever call my phone this early in the morning." Officer Moore yelled. He was pissed.

We both started laughing which only enraged

him more. Life was definitely going to be good, again.